SUMMERHOUSE

A DORLING KINDERSLEY BOOK

www.dk.com

First published in Great Britain in 1999
by Dorling Kindersley Limited,
9 Henrietta Street, London WC2E 8PS

2 4 6 8 10 9 7 5 3 1

A CIP catalogue record for this book is available from the British Library.

ISBN 0-7513-7191-2

Colour reproduction by Dot Gradations, UK
Printed and bound by Tien Wah Press, Singapore

SUMMERHOUSE

LAURENCE ANHOLT • ILLUSTRATED BY LYNNE RUSSELL

DORLING KINDERSLEY
LONDON • NEW YORK • STUTTGART • MOSCOW • SYDNEY
Visit us at www.dk.com

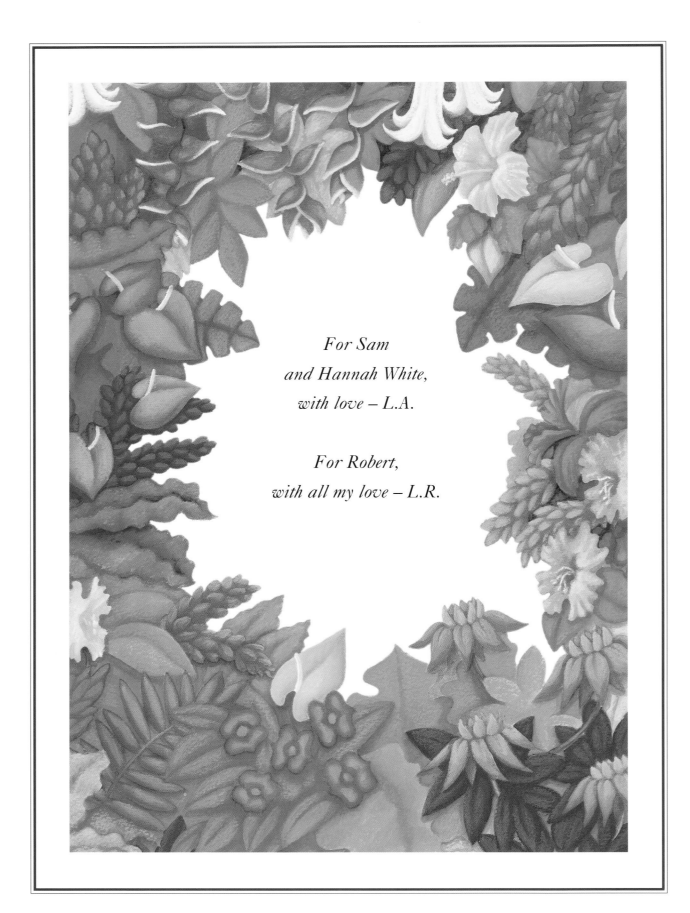

For Sam
and Hannah White,
with love – L.A.

For Robert,
with all my love – L.R.

W HEN ELLA'S GRANDMA LAUGHED, it started like a tiny tickle, deep down inside.

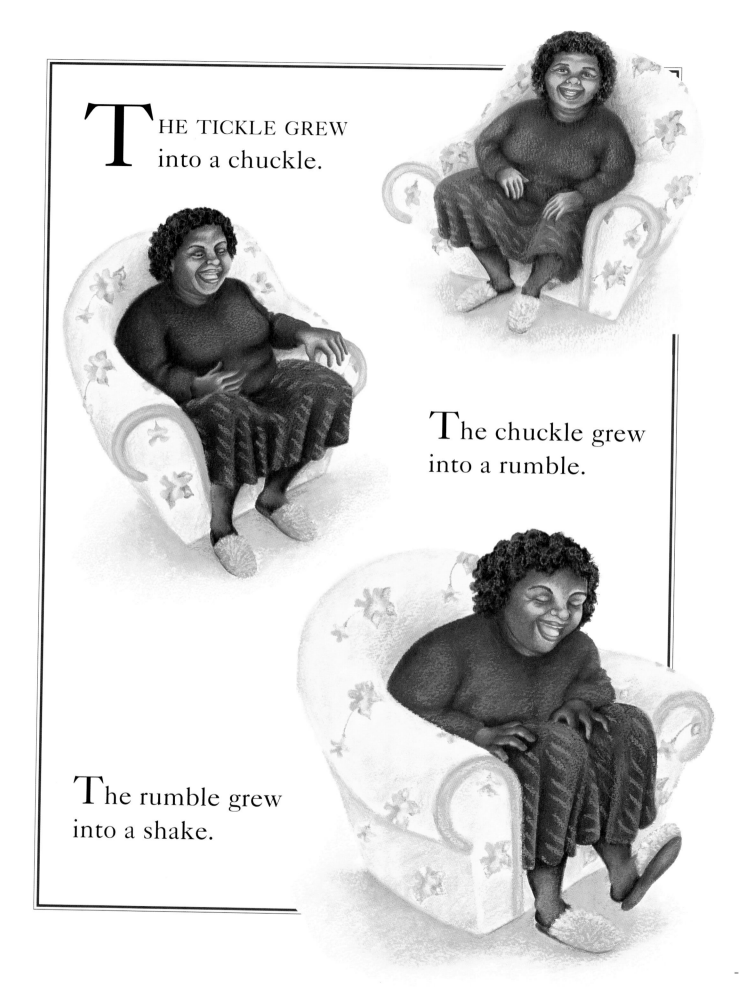

T HE TICKLE GREW
into a chuckle.

The chuckle grew
into a rumble.

The rumble grew
into a shake.

Then her whole big body began
to rock, until her face burst into
the biggest, loudest laugh that
anyone had ever heard.

And soon everyone
caught it – like
sneezes in winter.
And nobody could stop.
Not Ella's grampa
or Ella's mum,
or even Ella's dad.

But Ella didn't laugh.
Ella was a serious girl.

Although Ella loved her grandma,
she just didn't get the joke.

ELLA'S GRANDMA AND GRAMPA moved to this old house many years before Ella was even born. They had left their tiny island home and sailed to this big cold country so Grampa could find a job.

And the first thing Grampa had done
was to build a summerhouse for
Grandma at the end of the garden.
To remind her of the brightly-coloured
beach huts back home.

BUT THAT WAS A LONG TIME AGO. Now it was winter in this faraway town and Grampa's hair was as white as the snow on the summerhouse roof.

Now they all sat inside and listened to Grampa telling stories about their island home in the blue-green ocean.

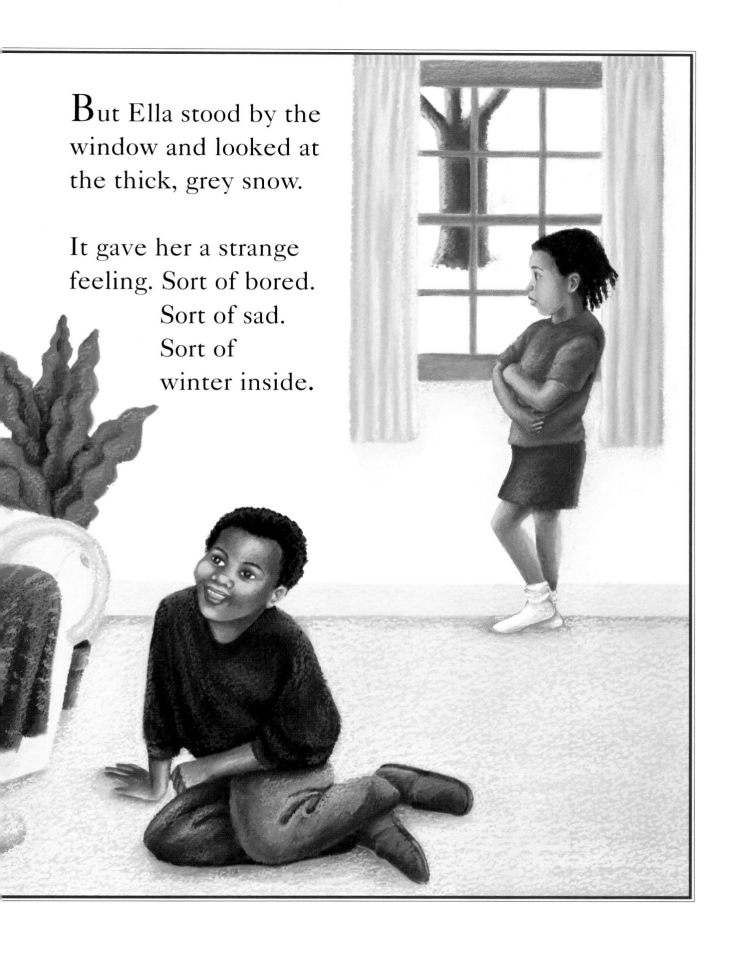

But Ella stood by the window and looked at the thick, grey snow.

It gave her a strange feeling. Sort of bored.
Sort of sad.
Sort of
winter inside.

ONE DAY, GRANDMA SAID, "Listen, Ella. You're too young to be so serious. You have to find some sunshine inside yourself – even when it's winter.

"That's why I'm so big," she grinned. "Because I have the WHOLE of the sun inside of me."

Grandma hugged her close. "Here's something for you, girl," she whispered, holding out a long brass key. "The key to the summerhouse. Now wrap up warm and run out to play."

THERE WERE NO OTHER FOOTPRINTS
in the silent garden as Ella walked
across the snow. She looked back at her family, who
were still laughing inside. She tried to find the
sunshine inside herself, but it just wasn't there.

Ella climbed the icy wooden steps to the summerhouse door and pushed the key in the lock. She turned the handle and shoved hard, but the door was frozen shut. So Ella kicked it hard.

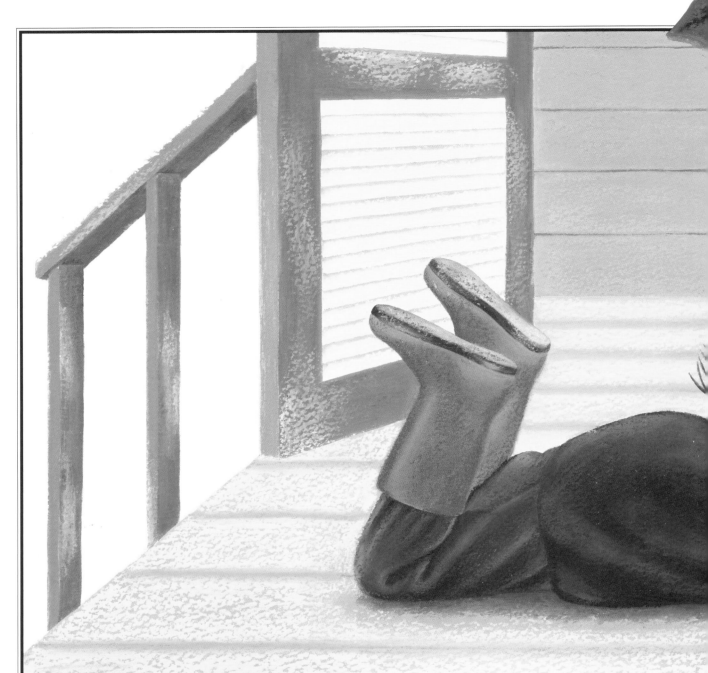

The door swung open just a little. Just a tiny crack. A warm light shone from inside.

Then the door burst open, and Ella fell right inside the summerhouse and tumbled onto the floor.

It was warm in there
and the noise was loud.
Sort of surf sighing.
Sort of sea birds crying.
Sort of palm leaves rustling.

Then Ella smelt a strange smell.
Sort of wild flowers.
Sort of coconut oil.
Sort of salty sand.

Then Ella felt a strange feeling.
Sort of warm wind blowing.
Sort of sunshine on skin.
Sort of summertime.

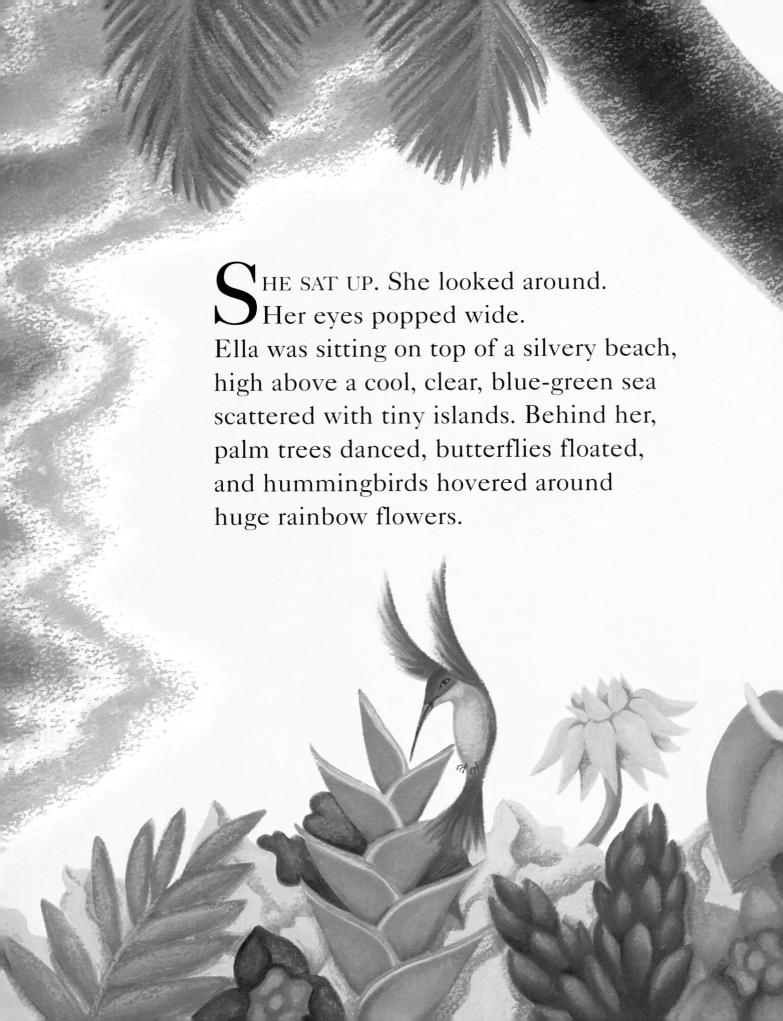

SHE SAT UP. She looked around.
Her eyes popped wide.
Ella was sitting on top of a silvery beach,
high above a cool, clear, blue-green sea
scattered with tiny islands. Behind her,
palm trees danced, butterflies floated,
and hummingbirds hovered around
huge rainbow flowers.

E LLA STOOD UP. She looked down at
her winter clothes and her big red boots.
And the smallest, tiniest smile crept across her face.

Ella pulled off her scarf and dropped it on the sand.

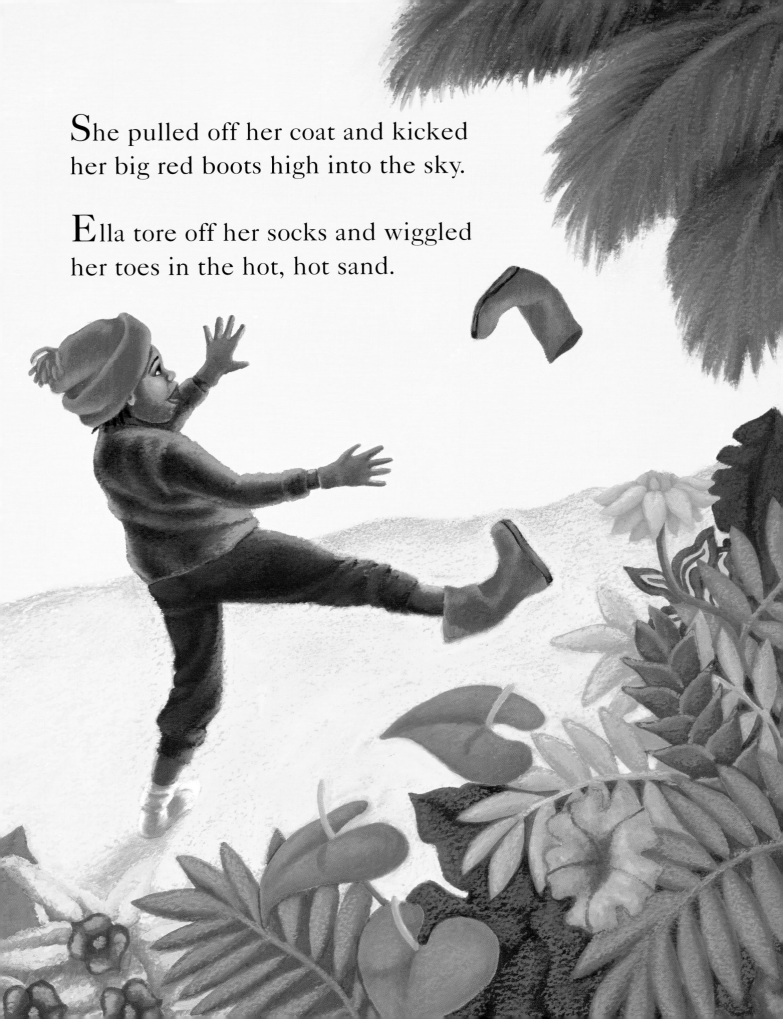

She pulled off her coat and kicked her big red boots high into the sky.

Ella tore off her socks and wiggled her toes in the hot, hot sand.

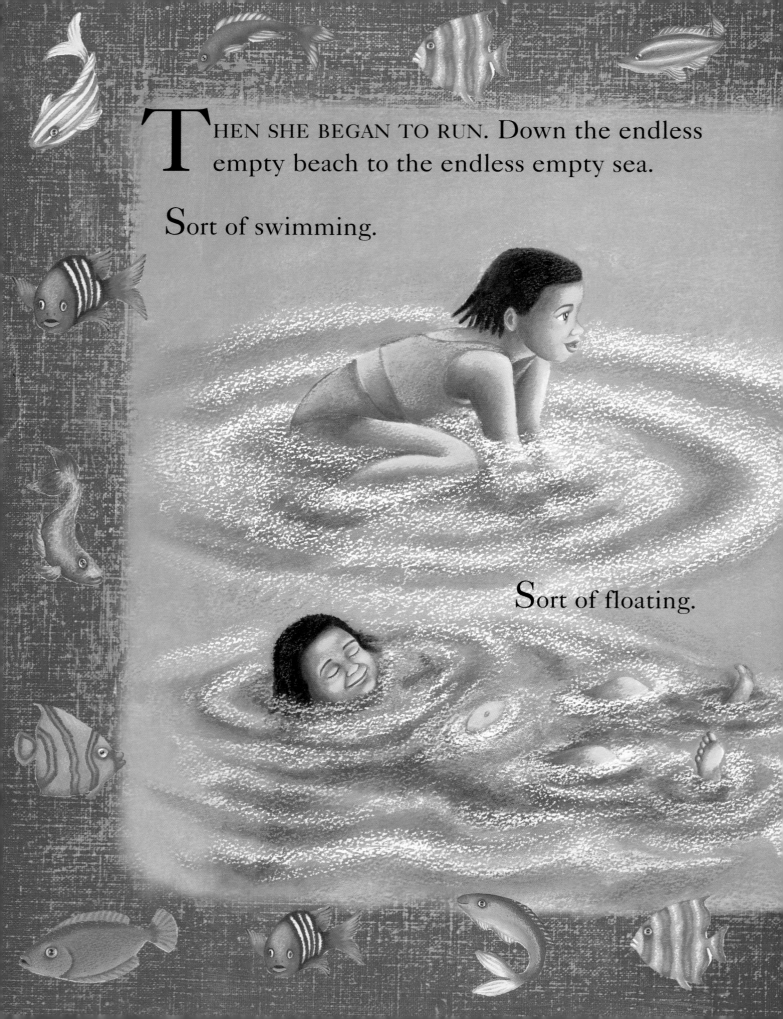

THEN SHE BEGAN TO RUN. Down the endless empty beach to the endless empty sea.

Sort of swimming.

Sort of floating.

Sort of diving.

Down, down,
deep as a dolphin,
then rushing and
bursting for air.

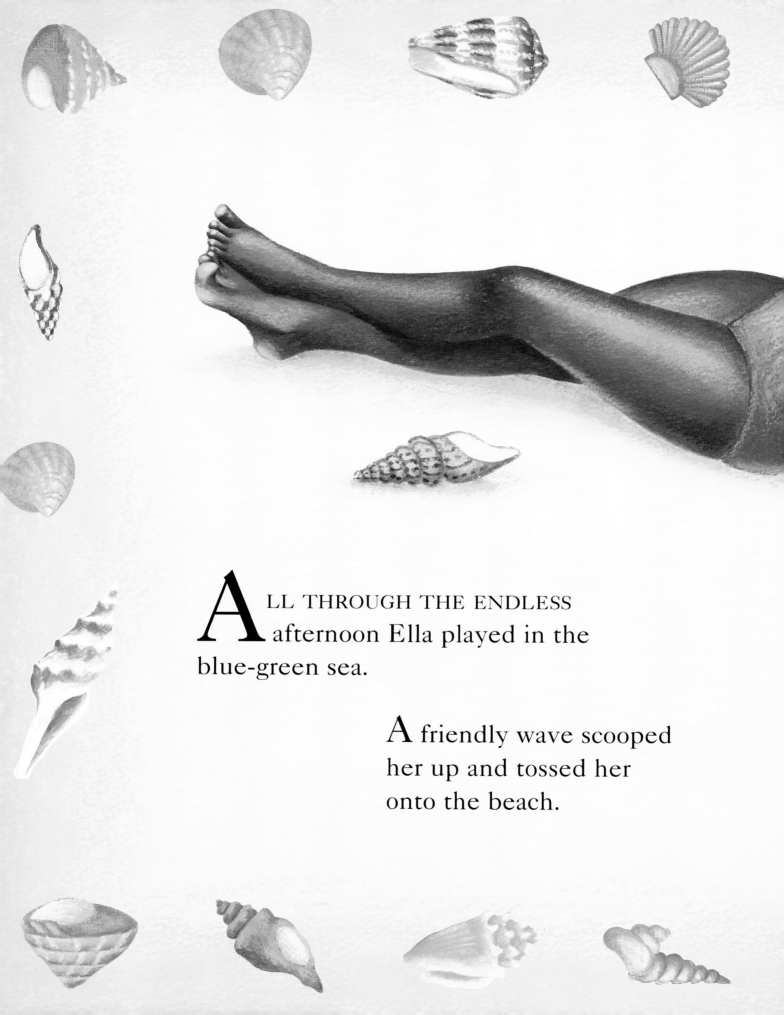

ALL THROUGH THE ENDLESS
afternoon Ella played in the
blue-green sea.

A friendly wave scooped
her up and tossed her
onto the beach.

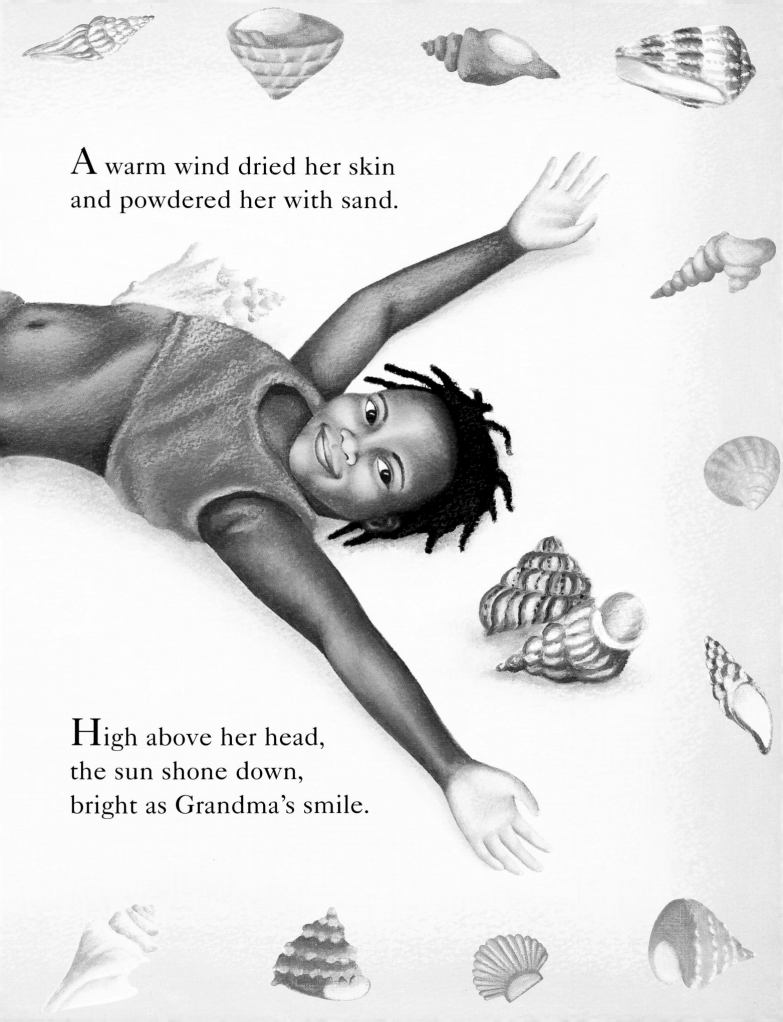

A warm wind dried her skin
and powdered her with sand.

High above her head,
the sun shone down,
bright as Grandma's smile.

So Ella didn't mind when it was time to go.
Now that she knew where the sunshine was,
she could come anytime she pleased.
She ran back to the summerhouse
and pulled on her winter clothes.

Then Ella closed the summerhouse door,
locked it carefully with the brass key, and
hurried through the snowy garden
back to Grandma's house.

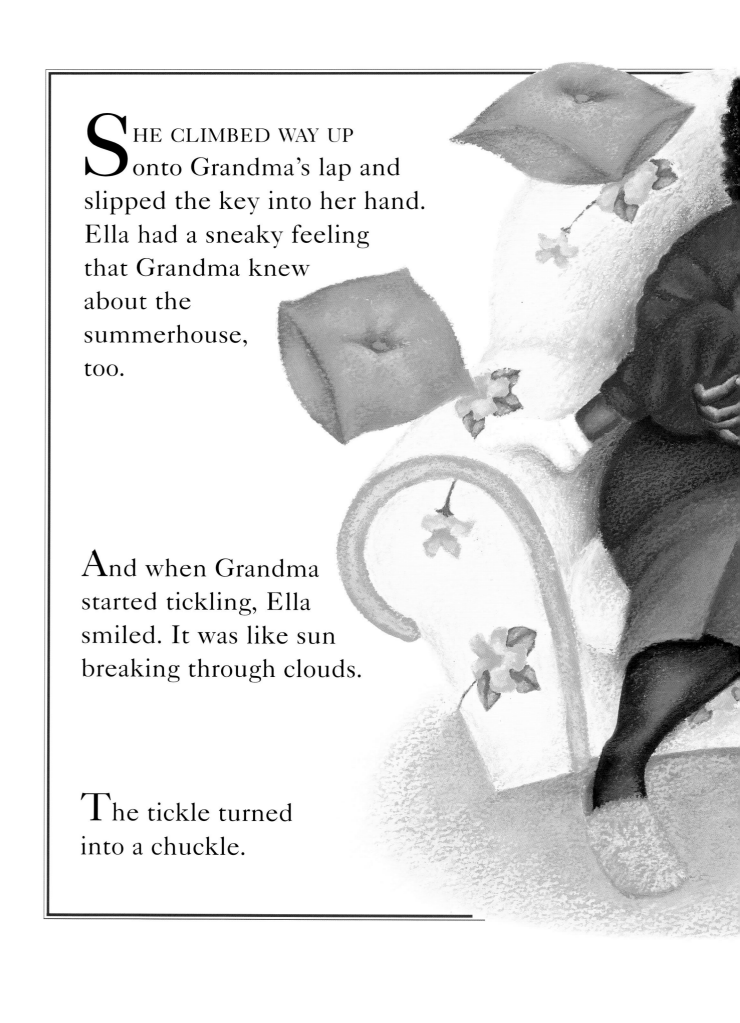

SHE CLIMBED WAY UP onto Grandma's lap and slipped the key into her hand. Ella had a sneaky feeling that Grandma knew about the summerhouse, too.

And when Grandma started tickling, Ella smiled. It was like sun breaking through clouds.

The tickle turned into a chuckle.

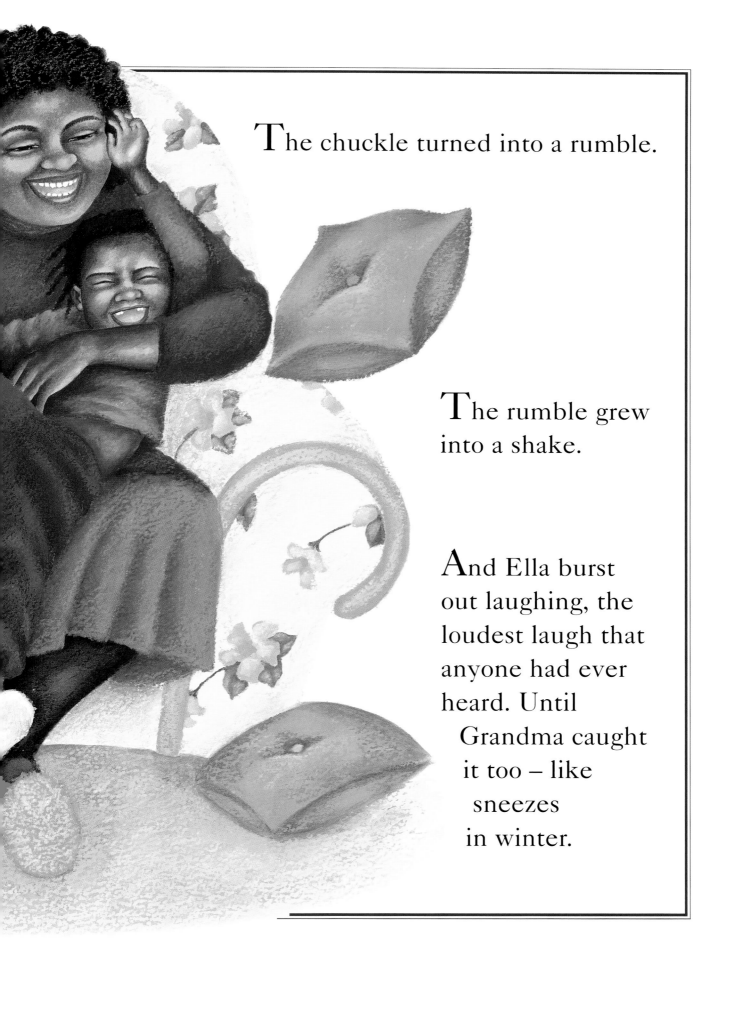

The chuckle turned into a rumble.

The rumble grew into a shake.

And Ella burst out laughing, the loudest laugh that anyone had ever heard. Until Grandma caught it too – like sneezes in winter.

AT LAST ELLA YAWNED and curled up small and fell fast asleep on Grandma's lap. She felt a warm new feeling somewhere deep, deep down.

Sort of summer in winter.
Sort of sunshine inside.
Sort of HAPPY.